P9-CRP-933

DATE DUE

MAY 0 7 1987 Ⓚ

11-10

FIRST GRADE

BRACEVILLE ELEMENTARY SCHOOL
DISTRICT #75
BRACEVILLE, ILLINOIS   60407

Tall Tales books bring to the primary reader stories filled with boisterous action, humor, and excitement. Some are based on folklore; others are pure fantasy.

All the books have colorful illustrations that capture to perfection the gay, carefree mood of the text.

Each author has created an imaginative, easy-to-read story designed to entice the reader into the magic realm of books.

The Old Witch Goes to the Ball

By Ida DeLage

Illustrations by Gustave E. Nebel

GARRARD PUBLISHING COMPANY
CHAMPAIGN, ILLINOIS

Copyright © 1969 by Ida DeLage
All rights reserved. Manufactured in the U.S.A.
Standard Book Number 8116-4055-8
Library of Congress Catalog Card Number: 69-15830

The Old Witch Goes to the Ball

"Whoa Lizzie,"
said the old farmer.
He stopped his car.
He read the sign
on the telephone pole.
"Say!" he said.
"Wait until I tell Ma!
Tonight's the night
of the Halloween ball!"

"Oh what fun, Pa," said Ma.
"Let's go to the ball!"
But what would they wear?
They thought and thought.
Then Pa saw the scarecrow
out in the cornfield.
"Ah ha!" said the old farmer.
"Now I know what I will be!"

The farmer's wife
looked in her cupboard
for some apple jelly.
"Ah ha!" said Ma.
"Now I know what I will be.
I'll be Old Mother Hubbard
who went to the cupboard."

Down in the valley
the wind began
to play some tricks.
"Whoo-oo-oo," it went.
It shook the trees.
It blew the leaves.
It pulled the sign
off the telephone pole.
The sign went up, up,
like a kite.
It flew over the valley
and up the hill.
It flew into the cave
where the old witch lived.

The old witch of the hill
was stirring her brew.
"What's this? Oh ho!"
she said.
The old witch caught the paper.
Then she read the sign.

"Ooo-oo-oo, how nice!"
said the old witch.
"A party!
No one ever invited me
to a party before.
Prizes too. How lovely!"
The old witch combed her hair.
She put on her best hat.
She put on her best cloak,
the one with no holes in it.
She even changed her socks.
Now she was ready to go.
The old witch could hardly wait
until eight o'clock.

Soon the moon peeped
over the hill.
Now it was eight o'clock!
The happy old witch
hopped on her broom.
She was on her way
to her very first party!

In the town hall
everything was ready.
All the people were coming
to the Halloween Ball.

The first one who came
was George Washington.
He was really Mike the mailman.
Then came Little Bo-Peep
and a big red devil.
They were the schoolteacher
and Pete the barber.

In came fourteen ghosts,
a pirate, a bride,
a frog, and a bunny.
Next came a scarecrow,
Old Mother Hubbard,
Little Red Riding Hood,
and . . . an old witch!

15

People looked at each other.
Everyone had on a mask.
"Who are you?" they asked.
"Who are you?"
But no one would tell.
"Guess who," they all said.
But everyone whispered,
"We all know
who that old witch is.
That's Grandma Petticoat.
She comes to the ball
dressed like a witch
every single year.
We always know her."

Now the fun began.

Jolly Jake took his fiddle.

He jumped up

on a big fat pumpkin.

"Cider in a jug,

Apple on a string.

Come on folks

Let's dance and sing.

Grab your partner

Two by two.

Make a circle and

Skip to my Lou."

Everyone ran around

to find a partner.

"If you can't find a redbird
A bluebird will do.
Skip to my Lou
My darlin'."

Then they danced
Shoo Fly,
Needle in the Haystack,
and Pop Goes the Weasel.

"Look!" everyone said.
"See how Grandma Petticoat
can dance.
You would never think
she's 102 years old!"

"All right folks,"
said Jolly Jake.
"Everyone line up.
Now it's time
for the grand march.
The judges will pick
the best costumes.
The first prize will be
this beautiful cake.
It has a surprise
in every piece."

Everyone lined up.

The grand march began.

Around and around they went.

The judges looked and looked.

It was hard to pick the winner.

Everyone said,
"Grandma Petticoat
will win the prize.
She looks just like
a real old witch."

Jolly Jake held up his hand.
"Listen everyone," he said.
"The judges are now ready
to give the prize.
The first prize goes to . . .
Little Red Riding Hood!"
Everyone clapped and clapped.
Little Red Riding Hood
took off her mask.
Who do you suppose it was?
It was Grandma Petticoat!
"I got tired of being a witch
every single year,"
said Grandma Petticoat.

"Well then," everyone said,
"who are you, old witch?
We thought you were
Grandma Petticoat!"
All of a sudden
there was a big puff of smoke!

Thirty-two mice began to run
all over the floor.
"Eee-ee-eek!"
screeched the ladies.
They jumped upon the chairs.
Big, fat toads were there!

27
BRACEVILLE ELEMENTARY SCHOOL
DISTRICT #75
BRACEVILLE, ILLINOIS 60407

Jolly Jake's fiddle bow
turned into rubber.
The cider turned into vinegar.
The apples were full of worms.
The donuts were full of ants.

There was a terrible screech
and a big flash of light.
Swish!
The old witch flew
out of the window!

"Oh-oh-oh."
everyone said.
"What was that?"
But the old farmer and his wife
knew what it was.
They ran out of the door
and jumped into their old car.
"Land sakes!" said the wife.
"That's the old witch
of the hill, for sure.
I know her tricks!
She's very angry
because she didn't win
the first prize."

"Hurry up, Pa.
We have to get home fast.
That old witch
will be around tonight,
and it won't be for any good!"

The old witch flew
back to her cave.
She made her fire.
She muttered and she sputtered.
"I will make some brew,"
she said.
"I'll fix everyone.
I'll put a spell
on the whole town.
I'll show them!
Huh! Who would want
that old cake anyway!
Silly old cake!
Huh!"

The old farmer
got his hayfork.
He sat down on the porch.
"I'll chase that old witch away
if she comes around here,"
he said.
"No, Pa," said his wife.
"I have a better plan."

The farmer's wife made a fire
in her stove.
She got the biggest pan
that would fit into her oven.
She baked a big, big cake.

When the cake was done
Ma poked a prize
in every piece.
She put in:
    A little bell
    Some nuts
    Some candy
    A little red ball
    A gold ring
    A safety pin
    A balloon to blow up
    A powder puff
    A lipstick
    A new cork for a jug.

Then the farmer's wife
made some beautiful frosting.
She put it all over the cake.
It said:

"HAPPY HALLOWEEN
OLD WITCH"

The farmer's wife
put the big cake
out on the back porch.
She was very careful
to bring the pussy cat
into the house.

Then the old farmer
and his wife
went to bed.
Pa was soon snoring,
but Ma got up
and peeked out of the window.

Sure enough!
It wasn't very long
before the old witch
came flying over the barn.
She had her jug of brew
under her arm.

"First," said the old witch,
"I'll fix the old farmer.
I'll put a spell
on his farm.
The silo will be a mile high.
The well will be full of frogs.
The nanny goat's beard
will be ten feet long.
The pigs will be
skinny as pencils.
The horse will have
a tail like a turkey.
The cows' horns
will start to toot."

"And then," said the witch,
"I'll fix the farmer's wife.
I'll make the pussy cat
bark like a dog.
I'll make the canary
quack like a duck.
Her apple jelly
will turn into soup.
All of her wash
will be tied up in knots."

Just then
the old witch saw something
on the back porch.
"What's that?" she said.
She flew down
to see what it was.

"Ooo-oo-oo! A cake!"
she said.
Then she read the words:
 "HAPPY HALLOWEEN
  OLD WITCH"
"For me?"
asked the old witch.
She nodded her head.
She rubbed her bony old hands
together.
"How lovely!
A Halloween cake just for me!"
She forgot all about
the tricks she was going to do.

The old witch
had a very hard time
flying on her broom
with her big cake.
But finally she got back
to her cave.

The old witch sat down.
She ate three pieces of cake.
She found three lovely prizes.
Oh, she was happy!

"Eee-ee! A Halloween ball
is lots of fun,"
said the old witch.
"It's almost as much fun
as casting a spell.
I hope I get invited
again next year.
But if I don't . . .
I'll show them!
I'll go anyway!
And the next time,
I'LL be . . .
Little Red Riding Hood!"

The bats and the owls
All sit and wait.
The children hide
And shiver and shake.
But where is that witch
Who flies so late?
She's back in her cave
Eating her cake!